Padma Shri Pran

Maurice Horn, the editor of World Encyclopedia of Comics, has described cartoonist PRAN as Walt Disney of India.

Entertaining generation after generation, his comics have been constant companion of all the growing youngsters providing fun and amusement through his famous characters like CHACHA CHAUDHARY, SABU, SHRIMATIJI, PINKI, BILLOO, RAMAN etc. More than 500 of his titles are selling well in the market, and numerous comic strips are regularly appearing in various newspapers. His CHACHA CHAUDHARY comics had already been adapted for a TV Serial, and ran continuously for 600 episodes on a premier channel.

Travelling widely over the globe, he delivers lectures at various International Conferences. He has also been honoured with 'People of The Year Award' by Limca Book of Records for popularizing comics. His comic book 'United We Stand' was released in 1983 by the then Prime Minister Mrs. Indira Gandhi, and is still very popular among children.

Publisher

HI UNCLE HAIRY!
HI PINKI!

YOUR UNCLE IS GOING TO RELAX IN THE LAWN. SO, DON'T TROUBLE HIM.
OK MOM

I'M GOING TO THE TERRACE. I'VE BROUGHT A SPECIAL PASTE FOR KUTKUT FROM THE MARKET.

I'LL MAKE THE DISH FROM THE PASTE AND GIVE HER.

SQUEEK !!
PET

SQUEEK!

I KNOW, YOU ARE SLURPING TO SEE YOUR SPECIAL DISH PASTE.

WAIT TILL I MAKE ITS PASTE. THEN I'LL GIVE IT TO YOU.

OH, WAIT! KUTKUT.

WAIT! OH!

OH! THE PASTE FELL ON THE HEAD OF SLEEPING UNCLE.

OH! KUTKUT! YOUR INTENTIONS SEEM SCARY.
SQUEEK!

NO, KUTKUT!

KUTKUT HAS JUMPED DOWN, BUT I CAN'T DO THAT.

I'LL GO DOWN THE STAIRS & STOP KUTKUT.

WAIT KUTKUT !

OH !

OH ! MY HAIR !

HI HEAVY UNCLE! WHERE ARE YOU GOING?
PINKI & ROLLER
I'M NOT GOING, RATHER I'M COMING FROM DR. SCARY'S CLINIC.
I VISITED HIM TO TAKE TREATMENT, AS I AM OBESE.
© PRAN'S FEATURES

HE SUGGESTED AN OPERATION. I WAS READY. BUT, DO YOU KNOW WHAT HAPPENED NEXT?

ON REACHING THE OPERATION THEATRE, DR. SCARY BROUGHT A GARLAND. I ASKED HIM WHY HE HAD BROUGHT IT ?
WHAT HAPPENED ?

HE SAID THAT THIS WOULD BE HIS FIRST OPERATION SO IF IT'S SUCCESSFUL THE GARLAND WAS FOR HIM. IF UNSUCCESSFUL THEN FOR ME.

ON HEARING THIS I RAN FROM THERE.
IT'S GOOD. OTHERWISE THE RESULT WOULD HAVE BEEN SCARY.

PINKI ! THERE DOESN'T SEEM TO BE ANY WAY OUT OF OBESITY. SOB-SOB?

POOR HEAVY UNCLE !

STADIUM
ACTUALLY OBESITY IS OF NO USE.

GOJI UNCLE, WHY ARE YOU SO TROUBLED ?
I GOT AN OPPORTUNITY TO MAKE THE PITCH FOR THE INTERNATIONAL CRICKET MATCH .

I GOT THE PITCH READY. BUT MY ROLLER GOT DESTROYED IN MAKING IT FLAT.

THE MATCH IS ABOUT TO BEGIN. IN BETWEEN IF THE ROLLER ISN'T USED ON THE PITCH, IT WOULD BE TROUBLESOME.
THEN ?

HOW CAN THE ROLLER BE USED ? IT'S NOT WORKING.

I THINK I'VE GOT A SOLUTION TO YOUR PROBLEM.

WHAT ?

YOU'LL GET TO KNOW SOON.
www.chachachaudhary.com

MEET HEAVY UNCLE.

HE'LL SOLVE YOUR PROBLEM.

HE'LL BE HAPPY THAT HE COULD HELP SOMEONE.

WOW! EVEN A ROLLER COULDN'T HAVE MADE THE PITCH THAT SMOOTHER.

PINKI SPECTACLES
OH MY GOD PINKI, WHOSE SPECTACLES ARE YOU WEARING ?
GRAND MOTHER'S.
I AM TAKING IT TO GET IT REPAIRED.

I'VE HEARD THAT NOTHING IS VISIBLE FROM SUCH A THICK LENSED GLASS.

IT'S WRONG, I CAN SEE.

THAT TOO ABSOLUTELY CLEAR.
OK, WHAT CAN YOU SEE ?

DARK NESS !
!!

PINKI WAIT !
YES, UNCLE.

IF YOU ARE GOING TO AN OPTICIAN THEN GET MY SPECTACLES REPAIRED.

GIMME.

IT SEEMS YOU ARE GOING TO AN OPTICIAN ! GET MY SPECS ALSO RECTIFIED !

I THINK YOU ARE GOING TO GET YOUR SPECS REPAIRED.
YES, BUT THE PAIN IN MY KNEES DOESN'T LET ME WALK.

GIVE YOUR SPECS TO ME, I'LL GET THEM REPAIRED.

THANKS ! PINKI !
PINKI ! TAKE MY SPECS ALSO.

SURE !
EVERYONE'S SPECS WOULD BE OK IN 1 HOUR. TILL THEN I'LL ROAM AROUND IN THE MALL.
MOLL
Glass
www.chachachaudhary.com

I GET IMMENSE PLEASURE IN HELPING OTHERS.
BBB
BBB
Glass
AFTER ONE HOUR
Glas
Glas

I'LL RETURN EVERYONE'S SPECS, THEN I'LL GO TO PLAY.

AFTER SOME TIME.
WHERE'S PINKI? WHOSE SPECS HAS SHE GIVEN TO ME?
MY SPECS WAS OF A DIFFERENT NUMBER. WHOSE SPECS HAS SHE GIVEN ME?
I CAN'T SEE ANYTHING.

SOB! SOB! TELL ME WHERE'S MY FAULT!

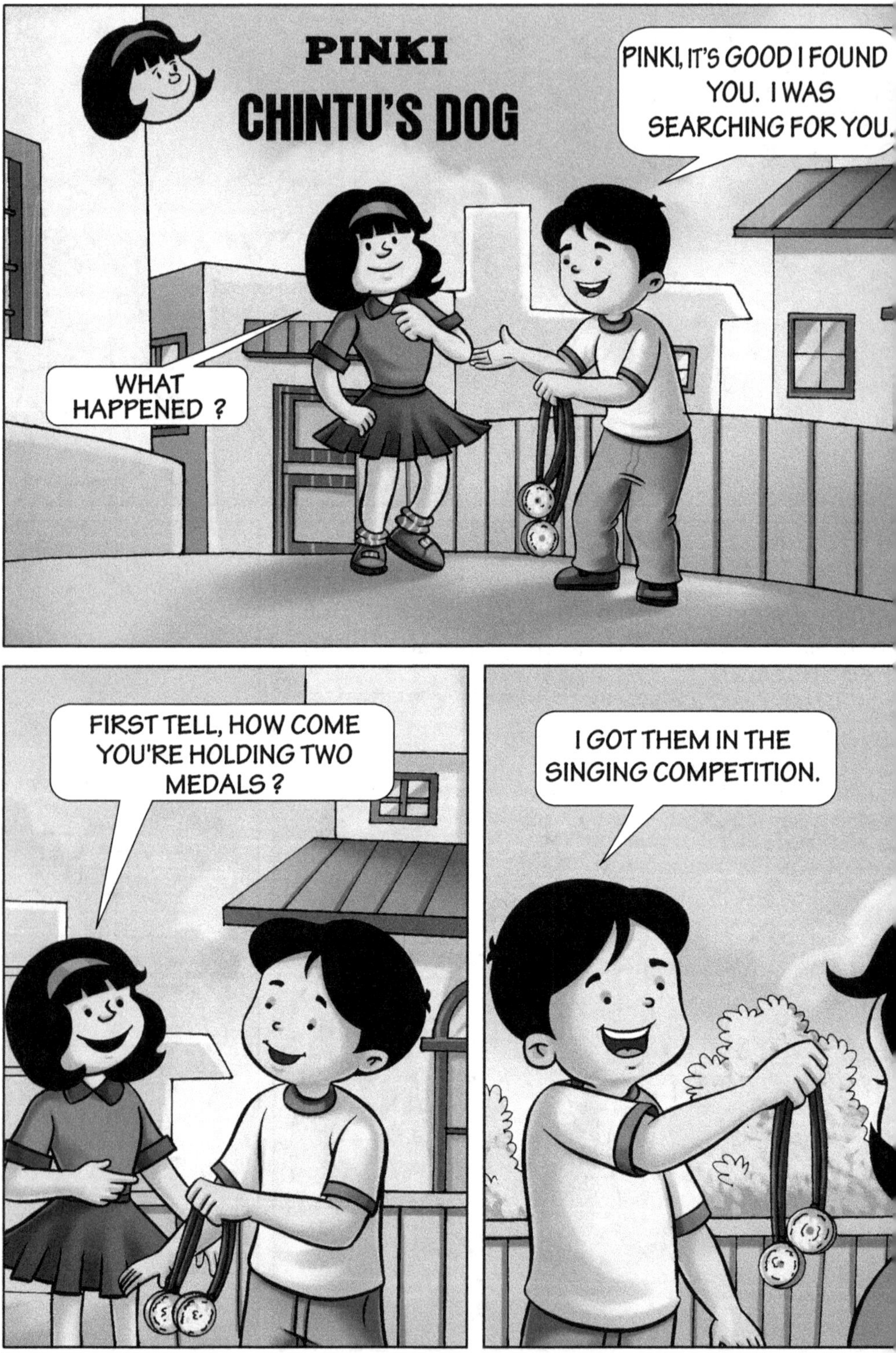

PINKI
CHINTU'S DOG

WOW! TWO MEDALS IN A SINGLE COMPETITION.

YOU MUST HAVE SUNG TWO VERY GOOD SONGS.

IT'S NOT THAT.
THEN?

I GOT ONE TO BEGIN SINGING.

SECOND TO END THE SAME SONG.
!!

ISN'T IT GOOD ?
VERY GOOD. NOW TELL, WHY WERE YOU HUNTING FOR ME?

MY UNCLE GIFTED ME A WONDERFUL PUP WHICH HAS GOT LOST.

HELP ME IN SEARCHING IT.
YOU MUST NOT HAVE TAKEN CARE OF IT, THAT IS WHY IT ESCAPED.

WE'LL GIVE AN ADVERTISEMENT IN THE LOST COLUMN OF THE NEWSPAPER FOR IT.

IT'S A GOOD IDEA, BUT NOTHING MUCH WOULD HAPPEN.
WHY ?

MY DOG WOULDN'T BE ABLE TO READ THE ADVERTISEMENT IN THE NEWSPAPER. HE CAN'T READ OR WRITE.

FORGET ALL THAT ! I'LL SEARCH YOUR DOG FOR YOU SOMEHOW. BUT I HOPE IT WON'T HAPPEN AGAIN.

YOU WRITE AN ESSAY ON A DOG SO THAT YOU UNDERSTAND HOW TO TAKE CARE OF IT.

OK! I'LL GO TO WRITE AN ESSAY ON A DOG.
I'LL GO TO SEARCH YOUR DOG.

THERE'S CHINTU'S DOG.
www.chachachaudhary.com

HE'LL BE HAPPY TO GET IT. I'LL GO TO HIM.

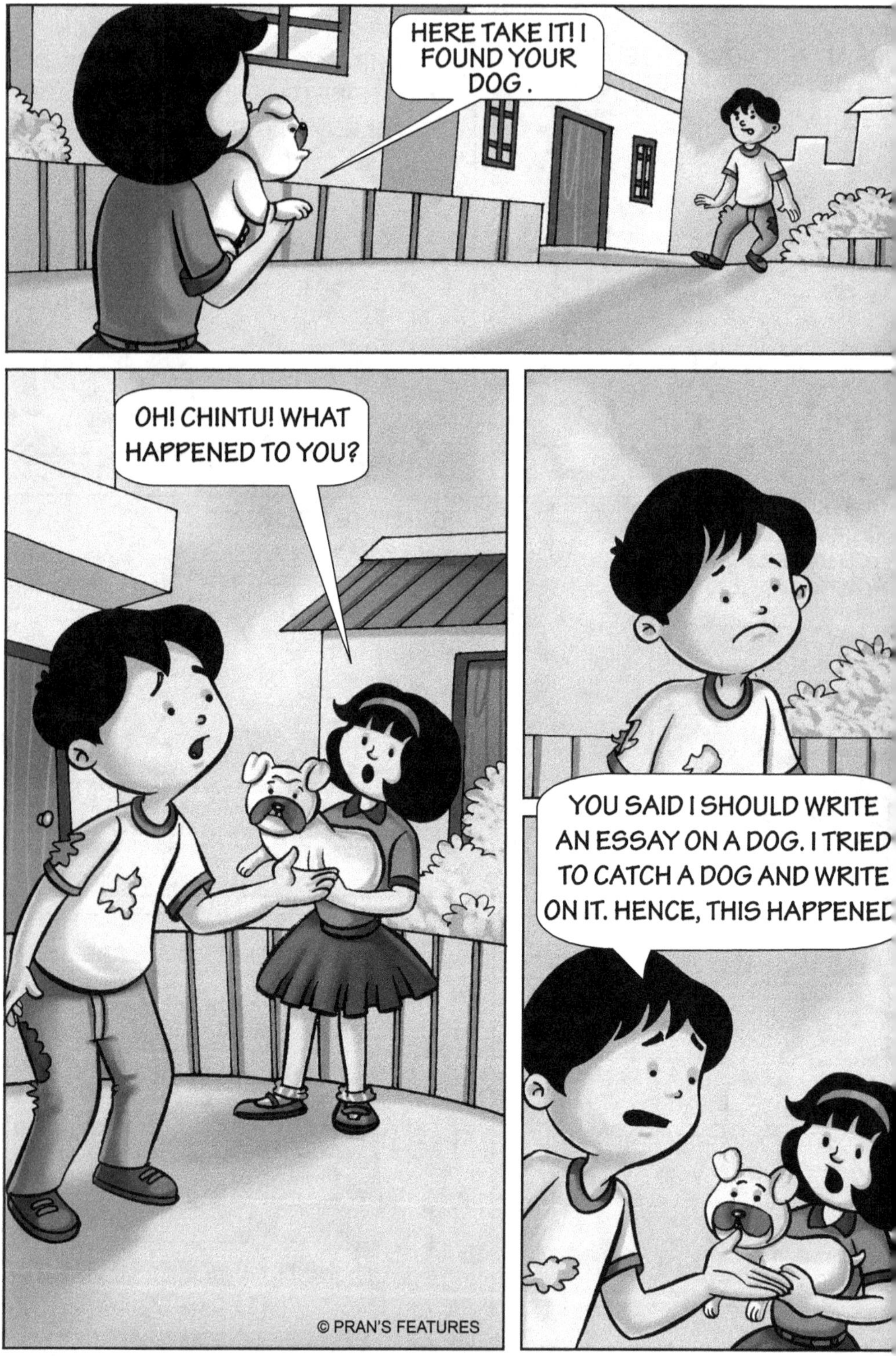

© PRAN'S FEATURES

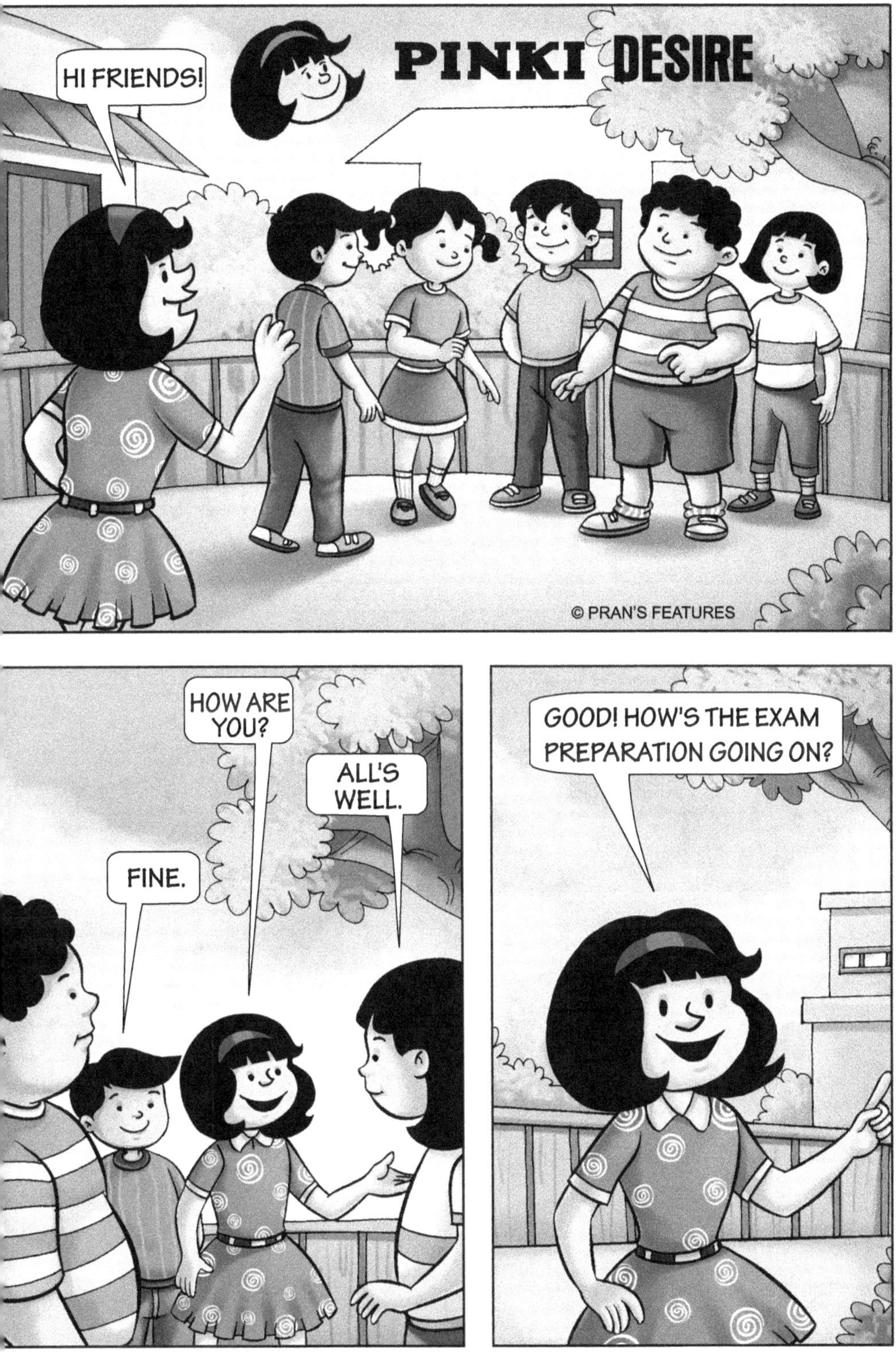

PINKI DESIRE

VERY GOOD. EXAM BOARD IS READY.

PEN'S READY.

PENCIL'S READY.

ABOVE ALL, EVEN THE DRESS IS READY.

ONLY THE REVISION IS LEFT.

DEVELOP SOME SERIOUSNESS TOWARDS YOUR STUDIES. IF WE'LL STUDY, ONLY THEN WE'LL BE ABLE TO FULFILL OUR DESIRES.

EVERYONE MUST HAVE SOME OR THE OTHER DESIRE.

WHY NOT? I WANT TO BE A DOCTOR.
I'LL BE AN ENGINEER.

YOU ALSO MUST BE HAVING SOME WISH, GABDU!

JUST SEE, ONE DAY I'LL GIVE A GOOD SLAP TO A LION.
www.chachachaudhary.com

LIKE THIS.

I'LL PULL A TIGER'S TAIL.

LIFT AN ELEPHANT.

AND THEN ROLL IT IN THE AIR AND THROW IT AWAY.

LIKE THIS.

VERY GOOD , YOU'LL SURELY DO THIS ONE DAY.

THE DAY YOU'LL DO THIS, IT'LL BE A DIFFERENT STORY.
WHAT?

THE OWNER OF THE LION, TIGER AND THE ELEPHANT TOYSHOP WILL TWIST YOUR EAR AND THROW YOU OUT.

25

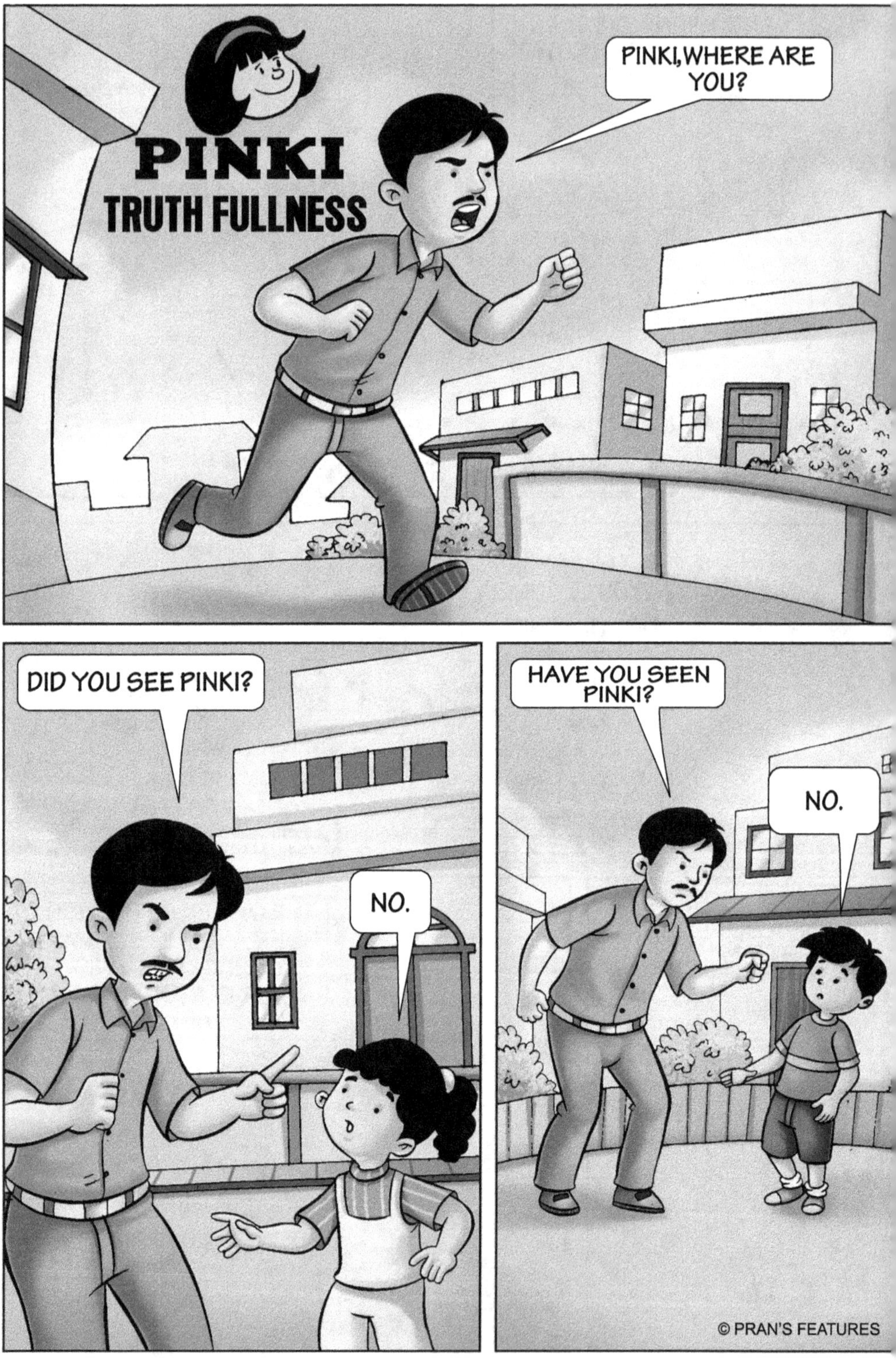

PINKI
TRUTH FULLNESS

WHY ARE YOU SEARCHING FOR HER, ANGRY UNCLE?
I'VE TO PULL HER EARS.

I AM HERE UNCLE. TELL ME WHY ARE YOU ANGRY?

A FEW DAYS AGO YOU TOLD ME THAT I SHOULD ALWAYS LAUGH.
OUCH! YES, I SAID THAT.

SINCE THEN I STARTED SMILING AND BURSTING INTO PEALS OF LAUGHTER.

DUE TO THIS THE ASYLUM PEOPLE CAUGHT ME.

I ESCAPED FROM THERE JUST NOW.
OUCH!

ALL THIS HAPPENED BECAUSE OF YOU.
OUCH! LEAVE MY EAR.

SORRY UNCLE! I CAUSED YOU MUCH TROUBLE.

COME ON, I'LL TELL YOU SOMETHING BETTER.

PRAY THAT ONE DAY YOU GOVERN THE ENTIRE WORLD ON YOUR FINGERS.

FINE NOW!

SHE'S A STRANGE GIRL. I HOPE SHE HASN'T MADE A FOOL OUT OF ME.

FTER FEW DAYS
www.chachachaudhary.com

HERE TAKE THESE SWEETS.

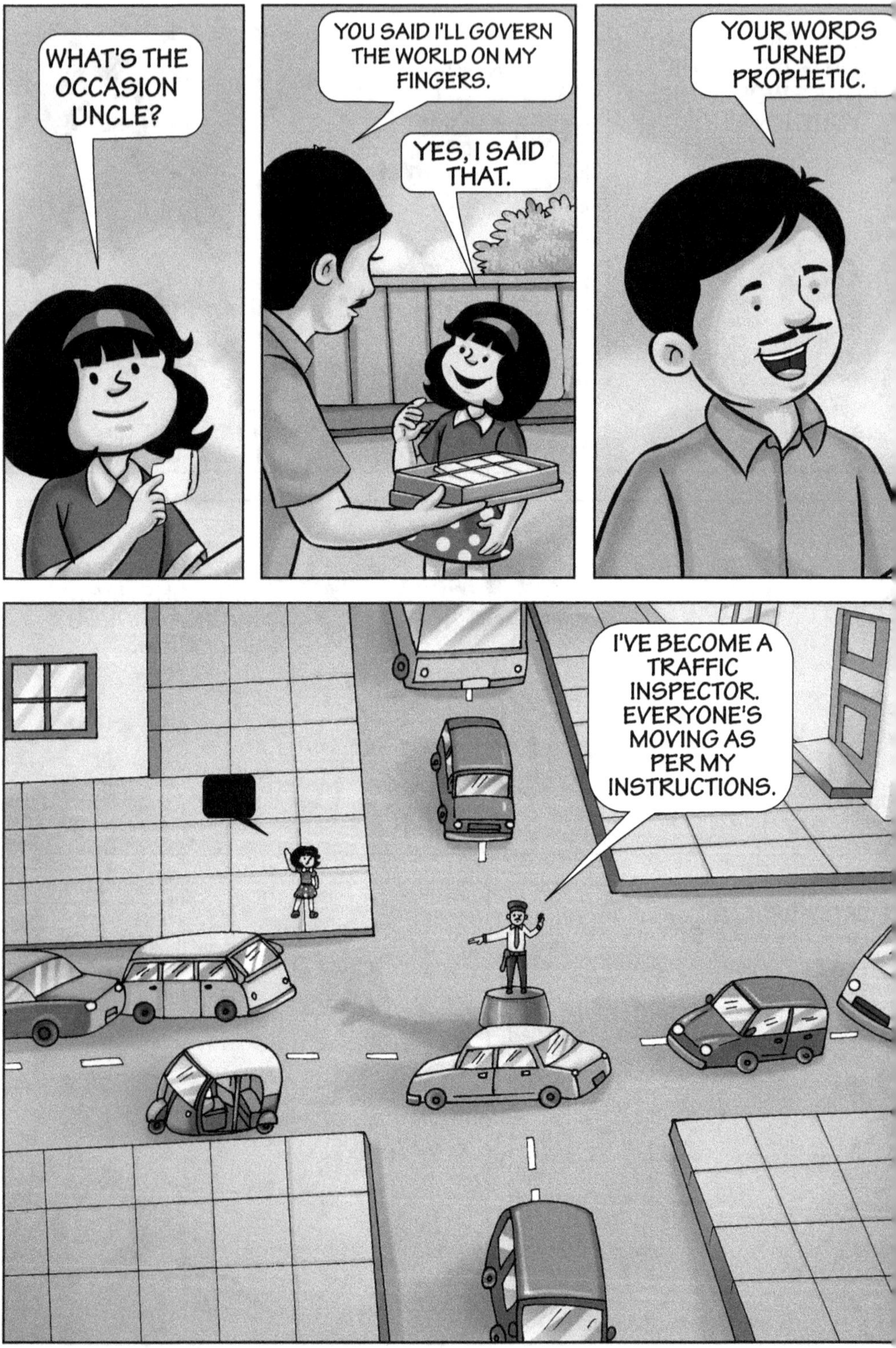

WHAT'S THE OCCASION UNCLE?

YOU SAID I'LL GOVERN THE WORLD ON MY FINGERS.
YES, I SAID THAT.

YOUR WORDS TURNED PROPHETIC.

I'VE BECOME A TRAFFIC INSPECTOR. EVERYONE'S MOVING AS PER MY INSTRUCTIONS.

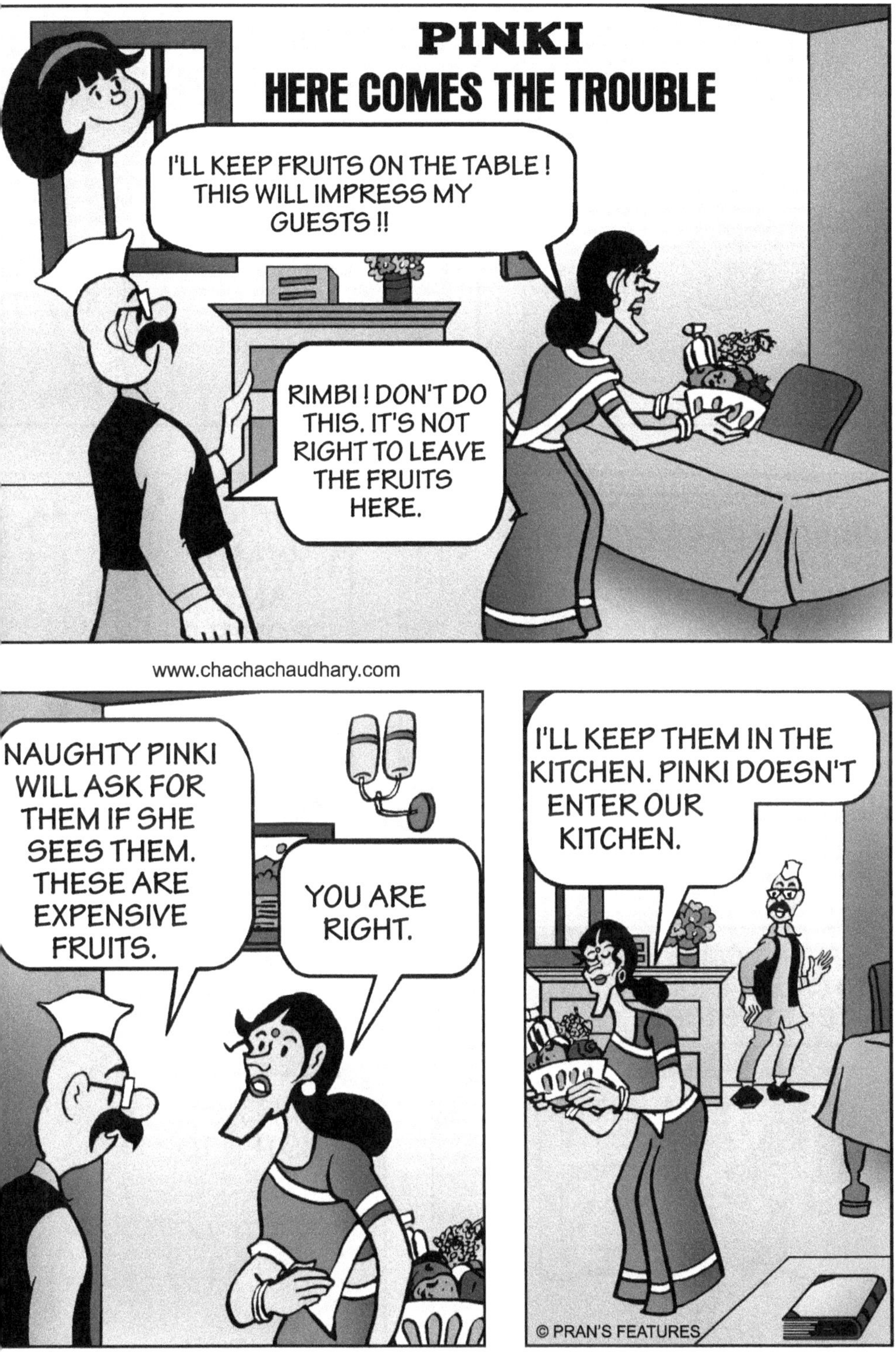

PINKI
HERE COMES THE TROUBLE

SHE WENT THERE.

JHAPAT UNCLE !
HERE COMES THE TROUBLE !

PINKI ! PLEASE GO BACK.

I DON'T WANT ANY TROUBLE.

I HAVEN'T COME HERE TO CAUSE TROUBLE, BUT TO STOP IT.

YOU ARE TRYING TO FOOL ME. I SAID GO !
AT LEAST LISTEN TO ME...

BE QUICK! SAY!
MY KUTKUT HAS ENTERED YOUR KITCHEN

SHE IS HUNGRY. I'M AFRAID SHE MAY EAT SOMETHING THERE.

OHH! FRUITS ARE KEPT THERE.

I WAS ALREADY AFRAID OF THIS.

OH WAIT! DON'T EAT OUR FRUITS.

JUST SHOO HER AWAY.
IT'S NO USE NOW.
GOBBLE !! GOBBLE !! GOBBLE !!

GOBBLE !! GOBBLE !! GOBBLE !!

KUTKUT ! LET'S GO.

YOU SEEM TO BE FULL NOW.

34

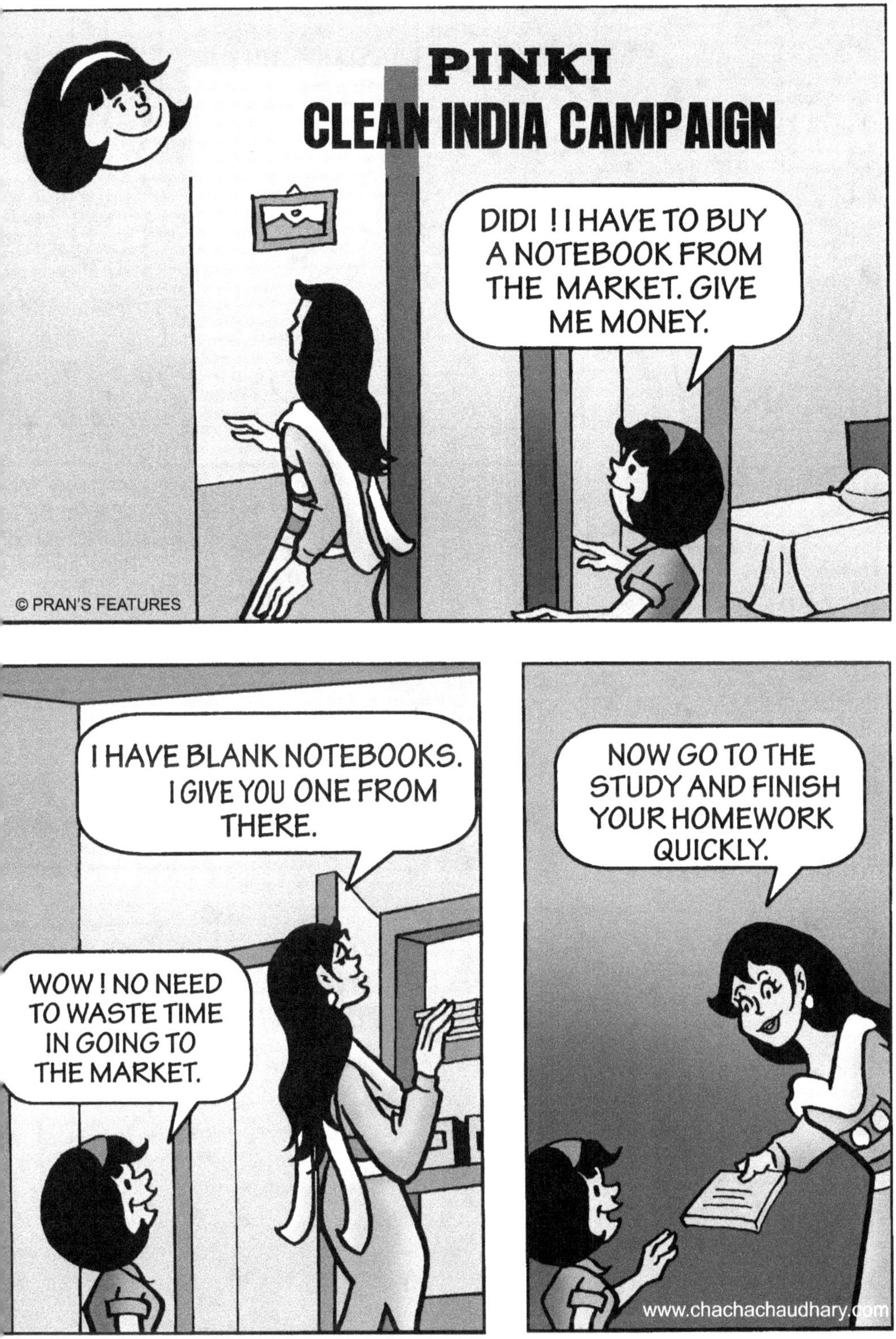

PINKI
CLEAN INDIA CAMPAIGN

35

PINKI ! YOU HAVE SPREAD SO MUCH MESS IN THE ROOM.

YOU ARE TEARING PAGES FROM THE NOTEBOOK AND THROWING AROUND !!
WRITING AN ESSAY, BUT UNABLE TO GET IMPRESSIVE LINES.

WHAT'S THE TOPIC FOR THE ESSAY ?
CLEAN INDIA CAMPAIGN !!

PINKI
JOHNY JOKER

HERE! TAKE MATAR PULAO.
THIS IS MY FAVOURITE DISH.

THIRD DAY.
YOU COME EVERYDAY. WHAT'S THE PROBLEM?

I AM A HUNGRY MAN. IF I COULD GET A JOB I WON'T COME HERE AGAIN.

OK. COME WITH ME. LET'S FIND WORK.

DIRECTOR UNCLE! WHY ARE YOU SAD?
I AM MAKING A TV SERIAL ON CIRCUS.

www.chachachaudhary.com

39

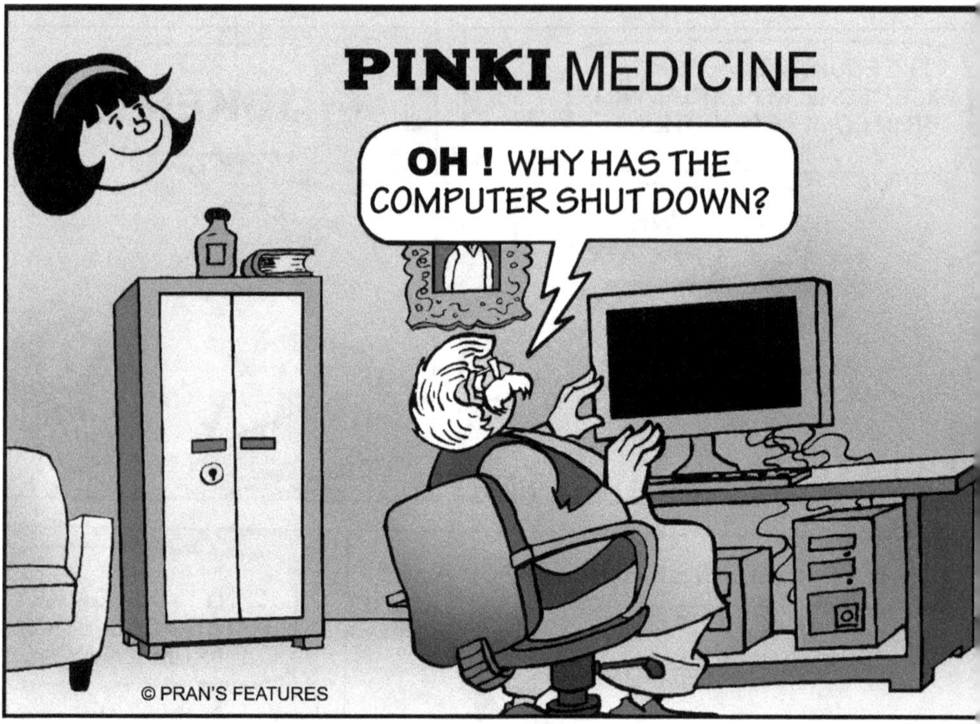

PINKI MEDICINE

WON'T THE COUNTRY FUNCTION IN THE ABSENCE OF PT. NEHRU ?

WHY ARE YOU SO ANGRY ?

HAD TO SEND IMPORTANT E-MAIL TO A FRIEND AND THE COMPUTER'S NOT WORKING.
THEN POST THE LETTER.

HE WILL THINK THAT I AM STILL LIVING IN THE STONE AGE.
BE CALM, YOUR BP WILL SHOOT UP.

HALF DONE WORK IS GIVING ME TENSION.

GIVE MY MEDICINE FOR BP.

IT'S KEPT IN THE OTHER ROOM. I'LL BRING IT.

CAN'T FIND IT. I THINK I'VE FORGOTTEN WHERE I KEPT IT.
HOW FORGETFULL !! YOU CAN'T EVER KEEP ANYTHING AT ITS PLACE !!

WHY IS THE ATMOSPHERE SO HOT TODAY?

ANOTHER TROUBLE COMES UP !

O AWAY, TODAY GRANDPA IS IN A SULLEN MOOD.
WHAT'S THE PROBLEM?

BP MEDICINE'S LOST AND COMPUTER WENT WRONG IMPORTANT MAIL HAD TO BE SENT.

GET THE MEDICINE FROM THE CHEMIST.

MY KNEES ARE PAINING, ELSE I WOULD'VE GOT IT.

YOUR KNEES HAVE CAUGHT RUST BY SITTING IN FRONT OF THE TV ALL DAY.
www.chachachaudhary.com

43

GRANDPA ! I HAVE A MEDICINE FOR PEACE.
ARE YOU A DOCTOR ?

HERE, TAKE THIS SWEET PAAN.

IT WILL KEEP YOUR MOUTH SHUT, ITS SWEETNESS WILL GIVE YOU PEACE.

NOW WITH A COOL MIND USE THE MOBILE NET TO SEND MESSAGE TO YOUR FRIEND TILL YOUR COMPUTER IS REPAIRED

ANGER GIVES PROBLEMS AND PEACE GIVES SOLUTIONS

BYE !
THIS GIRL WILL BECOME A PSYCHIATRIST ONE DAY.

FIND 10 DIFFERENCES

Find the differences in two Pictures and send us back to win a surprise prize - write down the
following details in block letter: Complete Name, Telephone Number with STD code (Mobile Number),
Age, Place of Birth, Date of Birth, Gender, Email ID and Complete Postal Address with Pin code.

Discover Talent @ Diamond Toons

X-30, Okhla Industrial Area, Phase-II, New Delhi-110020
Ph.: 011-40712100, 40712200, E-mail: sales@dpb.in

JOIN THE DOT

Draw a line from dot number 1 to dot number 2, then from dot number 2 to dot number 3, 3 to 4, and so on. Continue to join the dots until you have connected all the numbered dots. Then color the picture!

Join the dot and send us back to win a surprise prize - write down the following details in block letter: Complete Name, Telephone Number with STD code (Mobile Number), Age, Place of Birth, Date of Birth, Gender, Email ID and Complete Postal Address with Pin code.

FIND THE WAY

Help every duckling to find its own way to the little pond in the middle of the maze. send us back to win a surprise prize - write down the following details in block letter: Complete Name, Telephone Number with STD code (Mobile Number), Age, Place of Birth, Date of Birth, Gender, Email ID and Complete Postal Address with Pin code.

Celebrating !ndia

get invited to the festivals of India

The Great Indian Festival Series

Available in Hindi , English, Marathi , Bangla & Gujarati

X-30, Okhla Industrial Area Phase-II, New Delhi-110020, INDIA
Tel.: 40712200 E-mail: sales@dpb.in, Website: www.dpb.in

9 789384 906900